D0097239

HIDEAWAY
HOLLOW

HIDEAWAY HOLLOW

AND OTHER SPORTS STORIES
Compiled by the Editors
of
Highlights for Children

Compilation copyright © 1995 by Highlights for Children, Inc.
Contents copyright by Highlights for Children, Inc.
Published by Highlights for Children, Inc.
P.O. Box 18201
Columbus, Ohio 43218-0201
Printed in the United States of America

ISBN 0-87534-663-4

Highlights is a registered trademark of Highlights for Children, Inc.

CONTENTS

HIDEAWAY HOLLOW

By Donna Gamache

Frost covered every branch and twig on the ski slopes. There had been fog to start with, but the February sun had burned it away, leaving the hills postcard perfect. But Jamie, standing at the top of the steepest run, wasn't seeing today's view. He was seeing the ski hill last March, almost a year ago. That was the day he had collided with a tree on the Hideaway Hollow Run below and had broken his leg in two places.

7

He couldn't believe he was back at the top of Hideaway Hollow again. Why had he let his friend Skyla talk him into coming here? "You know the old saying," she had reminded him several times. "If you fall off a horse, you've got to get back on again, right away."

But Hideaway Hollow wasn't a horse. And Skyla wasn't the one who'd spent six weeks with her leg in traction and six more in a walking cast.

But she'd been so persistent. "Your leg is fine," she had reminded him. "The doctor said it would be as good as new, even stronger than before, isn't that right?" Finally, he'd given in to her begging and agreed to go skiing with her.

He'd started on the bunny hill, and he wished now he'd stayed there. Again it was Skyla's urging that had moved him. "You've been on this hill for half an hour," she had said. "Come with me on the chair lift to the top. You know this bunny hill is boring!"

It was, and he'd given in to her. He'd ridden to the top five times and had skied down four different slopes, and his leg did feel fine. He had worked out any stiffness on the steep slopes of Smoky Run and the moguls on Hilton's Hill. He'd even gone over a couple of jumps on Corgi's Cliff. The leg had performed well. The knot in his stomach had gone, though the feeling of flying hadn't returned yet.

Only this time up, Skyla had led the way to the top of Hideaway Hollow. The knot had returned and so had the fear.

He gazed out over the steep slope. There wasn't a whisper of wind today, not like a year ago when the strong south wind had melted some of the snow, leaving icy patches and bare spots. It was a grassy patch that had caught one of Jamie's skis, sending him out of control and into the tree.

But he shouldn't be thinking of that. "Put it out of your mind," his dad had said last night when Jamie confessed his fear. "When you stand at the top of that hill, just think about how you're getting down. Don't think of last year. That was just a freak accident."

"Right." Jamie had agreed then. But it was easier to convince yourself when you sat in your own living room than when you were on top of the very hill where the accident happened.

"There's lots of snow today," he reminded himself. "No bare patches to catch your skis." Somehow, that knowledge didn't help.

"You go first," Skyla suggested. She had waited for him, almost as if she could see into his mind.

He couldn't back out now, but he couldn't make his skis move forward, either.

"No," he said. "You go first. I'll follow you down."

She pushed off, and he stood alone at the top, watching her weave skillfully to the left and right, then schuss down the fast middle section of the run. She was good. *But I used to be, too*, he reminded himself, *when I still had my nerve.*

She was halfway down the hill, past the spot where he'd fallen last year, when suddenly—he couldn't see why—she appeared to lean over. She then nose-dived to the right, rolled over twice, and was still.

He looked back, then down. The only other skiers on this slope were far below. Any help for Skyla must come from him.

Pushing his fear away, he eased forward, slowly at first, then faster, faster. The slope was smooth. There were no bare patches and not many rough spots. In no time at all, he skidded to a stop beside his friend.

"Are you OK, Skyla?" he asked urgently.

For a moment he felt a sickening fear, and then Skyla turned her head sideways, brushing at the snow on her forehead.

"I'm . . I'm OK," she gasped, struggling to sit up. "Just—got the wind knocked out of me."

A wave of relief washed over him. "What made you fall?" he asked.

"My fault," she said, adjusting her hat. "Somebody—dropped a glove. I tried to pick it up—not too smart at that speed."

She brushed more snow away, and he helped her to her feet. "Everything looks all right," he said, checking her skis and bindings.

He glanced back up to the top of Hideaway Hollow, then down to the bottom again. The fear was gone.

"See you at the bottom," he grinned. And then he was gliding, gliding—flying once again.

ALL ABOUT WINNING

By Helen Kronberg

Kayla dragged herself out of the pool. "I think I may have a chance with the freestyle," she said. "But the backstroke is doing me in. It's going to make me look like a real dud."

"I don't know about that," said Susan. "But it sure doesn't look like you're having much fun."

Kayla looked at her friend as they headed for the showers. "Are you crazy? This isn't about having fun. It's about winning the meet." She was so tired she wished she could just forget the meet. But as she showered and dressed it haunted her every thought.

Kayla picked up her gym bag and started toward the door. "Did I improve at all today?"

"You were doing better before you started worrying about the meet," Susan told her. "It's like you've lost the rhythm."

"I wonder if I could bring in a tape player."

Susan shrugged. "Maybe . . . if you keep it far enough away from the pool."

The next morning, Kayla rang the bell at Susan's house while Susan was still at breakfast. "I've got the tape player," she said. "Let's go."

They arrived at the pool before it was open.

Kayla paced back and forth. "I can't wait to try swimming with the music," she said. "It's just got to help my rhythm."

As soon as the doors opened, the girls rushed inside. "You can't take that into the pool area," the attendant said, pointing to the tape player.

"But I want to practice to music," Kayla explained, her voice rising.

The attendant shook her head. "Rules are rules."

"I'll take it just outside the fence," Susan said. "With so few kids around, you'll be able to hear it from there."

Kayla nodded. "OK."

But soon the pool filled up. It got so noisy the music became only another distraction. Kayla got out of the pool and walked over to the fence. "How did I do?" she asked Susan.

"A little better."

Kayla sighed. "But it still isn't good enough, is it?"

"Probably not," Susan replied. She turned off the music. "I've got to run some errands for Mom this morning. Want to come?"

Kayla hurried to dress. She couldn't practice with all the kids around, anyway.

"I'm going to watch my cousin Jason at a swim meet sponsored by the Mayor's Office this afternoon," Susan said. "I promised I'd be there. Why don't you join us? It's really exciting to watch."

Kayla snapped her towel at a bug. Jason had cerebral palsy and couldn't walk very well. How could it possibly be exciting watching him struggle through the water? He couldn't have any chance of winning. On the other hand . . .

"I suppose he has as much chance as any of them," she said out loud. She turned to her friend. "Does he actually like competition?"

"He loves it," Susan replied.

Kayla smiled. "I'll be there. Jason's a really neat kid. I just wish he could be like other kids."

"In most ways he is like other kids." Susan turned up the walk to her house. "We'll pick you up about 1:30."

"OK," Kayla called.

Kayla was at the curb when Susan and her mother drove up.

"Jason called," Susan said. "He's so excited."

"I sure hope he wins," Kayla said.

They found good seats and waited for the event to start. Jason caught sight of the three of them from across the pool and waved. His smile seemed to include the whole world.

"He's just got to win," Kayla said. "If he doesn't, he'll be absolutely wiped out."

The contestants were being lined up. One of the kids fell into the pool, and they had to line up again. Then the whistle blew. They were off.

The place echoed with parents and friends yelling encouragement.

"I can't bear to look," Kayla said. "He's going to lose for sure."

Minutes passed, but as Jason climbed out of the pool, well behind the winners, he was still smiling.

"He sure is a good sport about it," Kayla said.

She lost sight of Jason for a while. Then she saw him on the sidelines, cheering for all the other kids.

At last he was lining up for his next event. "He's still smiling," Kayla said. "He doesn't look one bit worried about losing."

She cheered. She strained forward as if she could help him along. But he came out way behind. As the event ended, Kayla and Susan left their seats. Just before they reached Jason, Kayla saw him high five one of the other kids.

"What was that for?" she asked Jason. "That boy was dead last."

Jason nodded. "But he won," he said. "He made it all the way. He usually doesn't."

"Oh." Kayla watched as the boy greeted his parents. "I see."

"Congratulations," Susan said.

"Yeah," Kayla said slowly. "Did you hear us cheering for you?"

Jason laughed. "I was too busy to listen. But I'm glad you were here. Being in an event like this makes you do your very best."

"Competition is not so much about winning," Susan said. "Jason has already learned that."

Kayla nodded. *Maybe that's been my problem,* she thought. *I've gotten so uptight about losing, I can't let go and feel the joy of just doing my best.*

Kayla applauded as Jason and all the other participants received their medals.

17

Raley's Fish Story

By Patricia Shaffer

The present was long and skinny. Raley tore off the paper. Inside was the prettiest fishing rod he had ever seen. It had a shiny black handle and a silver reel. It had yards and yards of clear fishing line.

"Oooh!" Raley said. "Can I go fishing now?"

Dad smiled. "I'm afraid this rod will have to wait for spring."

Raley and Dad looked outside. Snow was piled high all around the house. "When is spring?" Raley asked.

"It won't be long now," Dad said.

Raley took his new fishing rod to the dinner table. He laid it across his lap. He took one bite of ham. He patted the fishing rod. He chewed his green beans. He patted the fishing rod. He drank his milk. He patted the fishing rod.

"If I shovel all the snow away, then will it be spring?" he asked.

Dad shook his head. "No. But spring will be here before you know it."

Raley took a deep breath and blew out the six candles on his birthday cake.

"What did you wish?" Mom asked.

"I wished spring would hurry up, so I can go fishing," Raley said.

That night Raley put his fishing rod on the floor right next to his bed. While he slept, he dreamed he caught a fish that sparkled like sunshine. It was as big as a whale.

"Is it spring now?" Raley asked in the morning.

"Not quite," Mom said. "But the snow is melting."

Raley climbed up on a chair and peeked out the window. He saw a big, big puddle in the middle of the driveway. That gave him an idea.

He ran upstairs. With the fishing rod in one hand, he stuck his right foot into his jeans, and then his left foot. He held the fishing rod under his chin while he buttoned his flannel shirt.

He gripped the fishing rod between his toes and ate his cereal in a flash.

Mom helped him pull on his red jacket, blue boots, and green mittens.

"Fishermen can usually dress themselves," he said to Mom. "But it's hard when they're holding a fishing rod."

"I understand," Mom said. She unfolded a paper clip and tied it on his line. "You can use this as a hook for now."

Raley ran out the door and into the yard. "I'm going to catch a fish for dinner," he called.

His boots squished through the mud. He dropped his line into the puddle. "Watch out, fish," he said. Taking teeny steps, he circled around the puddle, dragging the hook very slowly.

Suddenly the line grew tight.

Raley jumped. His eyes opened wide. "I did it! I did it!" he yelled.

"Did what?" Mom asked from the doorway.

"I caught a big—" He carefully reeled in the line. "I caught a big stick!"

Tangled in the line was a willow branch that had blown off the tree. "That is a big stick!" Mom said.

Raley nodded. He patted his fishing rod. If he could catch a big stick, he could catch a big fish. And he would, as soon as spring came.

MAGNET MAN

By Ellen A. Kelley

My eyes popped open. I checked my digital, glow-in-the-dark basketball clock: 4:00 A.M. Too early to get up. But not too early to worry. Today after school was our game with the Hornets. This afternoon, I'd be facing their 6'1" guard. I'd be facing . . . Magnet Man.

My bedroom was dark, but I saw Magnet Man in every corner. I saw his bean-pole body looming over me. I saw his huge hands reaching back to make sure I was trapped behind him.

Magnet Man is like superglue. Once he gloms onto you, there's no getting rid of him. You can't move. You might as well be stuck in quicksand. It's impossible to get open. You can't pass, and you can't shoot the ball.

Thinking of Magnet tied my mind in knots.

It made me grit my teeth.

It made me want to scream in four-digit decibels.

"Theo! What's wrong?" my mom asked, rushing into my room.

"Nothing," I answered. "What are you doing here? It's the middle of the night."

"Exactly," said Dad, peering in with half-shut eyes. "And you were screeching like a banshee."

"Uh, sorry. I was just . . . visualizing today's game. Coach Norton says we should visualize."

"We never visualized," said my dad, yawning. "We sweated. Kids today are afraid to sweat."

"I don't mind sweating," I said. "But Magnet Man won't let me. I can't move a millimeter while he's guarding me."

"We'll discuss this later," said Mom. "Try to get some more sleep."

I did, and I was late for school. Mr. Ralston, the toughest seventh-grade teacher in Washington Junior High, made me stay after to clean out the coat closet.

"I have a game," I protested.

He ignored me. "Everyone must take home his or her lunch bags, backpacks, and jackets," he ordered. "Smells like something died back here."

Actually, it smelled like several things had died—things like month-old tuna sandwiches and ancient milk.

Kids grabbed their stuff in a hurry and left me all alone with the mess. I threw away trash, hung up sweat shirts, and found my backpack, which had been lost for a week. It was stashed underneath someone's fuzzy blue sweater, and it smelled as bad as the rest of the closet. I grabbed it and ran for the gym.

Both teams were warming up. I shoved my backpack under the bench and found my friend Ricardo. "Maybe the Magnet is sick today," I told him. "Maybe he scraped his head on the ceiling and can't play."

"Stop dreaming," said Ricardo, laughing. "There he is now."

Magnet was practicing three-pointers. His lanky arms snaked toward the basket. His huge paws covered the entire ball.

"Magnet's looking good," said Ricardo.

"Too good," I said. "Just pray they don't do man-to-man defense, or I'll score zilch."

"Come on," said Ricardo. "Game time."

For a while, it seemed my prayers were answered. The Hornets played zone defense most of the game. We held our own, and at the third quarter's end, we trailed by only five points.

In the fourth quarter we hustled and tied it up with two minutes left. "We could win this," said Ricardo, checking the scoreboard.

"I know," I said. "Let's go!" We were revved up with the taste of possible victory. But then the Hornets' coach switched to man-to-man defense. Guess who was guarding me?

Magnet Man slowed me down. I sputtered like a sick pickup. Magnet was the gum on my shoe. I turned right. I whirled left. But I couldn't shake him off. Nobody could pass to me with Magnet Man in the way.

Coach Norton looked grim. He grabbed his clipboard. "Time out!" he called.

We headed for the bench. I opened my back-pack and plunged my hand inside to get my towel. Instead, I found an elderly hard-boiled egg! Phew! The awful smell punched me in the nose. I gagged. My hand was smeared with the gooey stuff. I wiped my fingers on my shorts, but I couldn't get rid of the smell.

"Go get 'em!" yelled Coach Norton.

My view of the court, the hoop, and the entire planet was blocked again by Magnet. But instead of getting closer, Magnet kept backing away.

He spun around, mouth gaping. "Whatta stink!" he gasped, running away from me. I wanted to laugh but there wasn't time.

I was alone beneath the basket. Ricardo saw me open and passed the ball. I shot.

Made it.

The buzzer buzzed.

We won, 40-38.

"Great play, Theo," said Coach Norton, coming over to me. Then his smile turned sour. "Phew! Better go home and shower, ASAP!" he added.

"Right, coach," I answered.

I ran back to the team. "We did it!" said Ricardo, grinning at me.

We ran the high-five line past the Hornets. When Magnet jogged by, he held his nose.

"What's the matter with him?" Ricardo asked.

"Nose trouble," I said. "It's ruining his game."

The Champions

By Margaret Springer

Janey adjusted her face mask and moved her catcher's mitt into position. This final game was almost over. Her legs ached. It was getting late, and her eyes felt tired. *Pay attention,* she told herself. *We can still be the champions.*

In the bright lights of the softball diamond, the Tri-Tec Rockets' pitcher, MaryBeth, was getting ready. "You can do it!" Janey shouted as she gave the signal.

The game had seesawed back and forth. After the sixth inning, the Rockets were ahead, 6-5. But now, at the bottom of the seventh and final inning, the Stars were at bat. With two out, they had runners on second and third.

"Take 'em home, Patsy," the Stars' coach yelled.

Patsy grinned and nodded.

Why did those Stars think they were so good? thought Janey.

The ball flew toward home plate. Janey was ready for it. But Patsy hit a solid grounder that bounced through the infield.

At that moment, the lights went out.

A groan went up from the crowd.

"Time out!" shouted the umpire.

"I can't believe this," Janey said.

"It's too dark to play," said the umpire. "So the game's called."

Janey and the others milled around Coach Riley.

"No problem," Coach told them. "The league officials will accept the score at the end of the last inning. That means we're the champions!"

"All right!" They gave each other high fives.

"We'll get the trophy in a few days," Coach said. "Well done, Rockets."

"Now we can have our victory party, Mary-Beth," Janey said, "at Dino's Pizza!"

"Why are you two looking so smug?" asked Patsy as she walked by.

"We won," Janey said. "Coach said so."

"No way," said Patsy. "We were winning. Anna was almost home, and Marcie was right behind her."

"How do you know you're not out?" MaryBeth challenged. "We would have thrown you out at first for sure."

"Some trick," said Patsy. "You can't win fair and square, so you turn off the lights."

"We never did. The power went out, and it's going to take time to fix," replied MaryBeth.

"Some trick," said Patsy again.

"That Patsy," said Janey. "Just because her dad owns Triple Star Cleaners, she thinks she owns the Triple Star team."

"Don't worry," MaryBeth said. "Your mom will give it to us, like Coach said."

In the twilight, Janey saw Mom, surrounded by team officials and parents.

"Well, that's what I get for being president of Girls' Minor League Softball this year," Mom sighed on the drive home. "I'll have to study the rule books on this one."

"But we won, didn't we? Coach said so," Janey cried to her mother.

"Don't be too sure."

Janey and MaryBeth planned the victory party at Dino's anyway.

The next day, Mom met with the league's executives and team coaches. She was busy with phone calls and rule books. Finally, she called a meeting of both teams. She wouldn't tell Janey anything ahead of time.

"We're going to reschedule the game, beginning in daylight, exactly where the last game left off," she announced.

Coach Riley was on his feet. "But Rule 5, Section 3c says—"

"That's for a regulation game, Jim. This is different. It's a championship game. The way I see it, we follow the exception under Section 3g."

"But—"

"We'll finish the game on Wednesday at 6:30," Mom said. "Any other questions?"

"But Patsy had just hit the ball," MaryBeth pointed out. "How can we go back to that exact same moment?"

"We'll do our best to be fair," Mom said.

Janey frowned. Mom looked so cool and in control. Coach Riley led his team outside. His face was red, and the veins bulged at the side of his face.

"We don't need to play again," said MaryBeth.

"It's not fair. We were winning," said Krista. "That should be counted as a regulation game."

"We want justice," someone else said.

"So let's not go," said MaryBeth. "I say we boycott the extra game."

"Yeah, we'll wear our team uniforms and have a pizza party that night instead," Krista said.

"Now, girls," said Coach. "I disagree. We need to follow the league rules. Besides, we still have a chance to win."

The girls looked at Janey.

"What do you think, Janey?" MaryBeth asked.

Janey hesitated. "I think we should boycott."

Coach Riley shook his head and sighed.

"We're not playing," Janey told Mom later. "We're going to Dino's instead."

Mom's eyes widened. "The Stars will win by default. It'll count 7-0 against you."

"We know that," Janey said.

"Oh, Janey," sighed Mom.

Wednesday came.

Janey's stomach felt tight as she rode her bike to Dino's. She thought of smug Patty and her team. No more softball till next season. It didn't seem right, somehow. She slowed her pace.

At the restaurant, the others were arriving. "Hey, guys," Janey said. "I've got a better idea. We're the

Tri-Tec Rockets, right? We're a good team, even though we don't always win."

The others had been thinking about it, too.

Janey was glad they had worn their uniforms. They got to the ball field just in time.

It was all over, of course, in a couple of minutes. Patsy was safe on first. Anna and Marcie raced home. Seven to six. Game over. The Stars leaped and cheered.

The Stars lined up on the third-base line. Janey watched as Mom presented them with the trophy for the third straight year.

It didn't feel good. But it felt better than not being there.

"Now let's go back to Dino's," said Janey.

"There's nothing to celebrate," said MaryBeth.

"Sure there is." Janey looked at Coach. He was shaking hands with Mom and with the Stars' coach. "Sure there is. We can celebrate being good sports," Janey said.

The Thinking Game

By Crosby G. Holden

Scott Dawson stared across the tennis net at the boy in the opposite court. He swallowed nervously. The boy looked older than ten, but Scott knew he wasn't. His name was Larry "Something." Scott had forgotten his opponent's last name almost as soon as he heard it. Larry Something grinned at Scott. Scott could almost read his mind: "Soft touch—two quick sets and it's over." A trickle of sweat ran down Scott's back.

Scott wished Coach Russo hadn't entered him in the junior bracket of the city tournament. He'd told him about it while they were walking from the clubhouse to the courts after watching Larry practice. The coach had put his arm across Scott's slight shoulders.

"You'll do all right," he said. "Just remember, tennis isn't all power. It's finesse, too . . . a mind game . . . looking for weaknesses and playing to them."

Oh, sure, Scott thought. *Some mind game! Tell that to the tennis ball.* He'd watched the pros play, slamming the ball hard at each other. And Larry seemed to hit almost as hard. Scott felt like David going up against Goliath, except he didn't have a sling. All he had was a midsize tennis racquet.

Larry won the racquet spin and elected to serve. He grinned at Scott.

"Nothing like starting with a winning game," he said over his shoulder.

Scott walked to the baseline. He waited for the serve, knees bent, racquet extended. His hands were slippery with sweat.

Larry's first serve boomed down the middle. Scott lunged to his left, barely touching the ball with his racquet frame. The next two serves were out of his reach. Larry served out the game with an explosive ace.

As they changed courts, Larry grinned at his opponent. "Tell me if you want me to take a little off my serve," he prodded.

Scott gritted his teeth angrily. His heart pounded as he got ready to serve. The net looked ten feet high. He double faulted twice. Then, his serve, which was usually his best weapon, became tentative. He pushed the next two balls over the net. Larry drove them deep for easy points. He grinned at Scott and winked.

By the time he was down three games, Scott was desperate. He caught Coach Russo's eye and shrugged helplessly. Coach smiled and tapped his head with his forefinger. *Think!* Scott wondered angrily. *What's there to think about?*

For the moment, he forgot about being nervous. His first two serves popped in sharply and he won both points. Then, he lost the next two as Larry ran around his backhand and drove two winners deep into the corner. Scott hesitated as he got ready to serve at deuce. Larry was standing tight to the center line. He had done that the first time Scott had served, too.

Scott moved a step to his right and served wide to Larry's forehand. Larry was late getting to it and tapped it back weakly. Scott volleyed it into the open court for an easy point. When Scott served for the last point of the game, Larry moved close to the double line. This time Scott moved to his left and served wide again to Larry's backhand. Larry popped up a weak return and Scott won point and game.

The rest of the first set ended quickly. Larry finally won, 6-4. As they sipped water and rested between sets, Larry said, "You got lucky that time, Dawson. Here's where I really turn it on."

However, Scott noticed Larry wasn't smiling quite as much anymore. Scott ignored him and walked to the far end of the court to think. *"It's a mind game,"* Coach Russo had said. *"Play to your opponent's weaknesses."* Maybe grinning was Larry's way to aggravate his opponent and put him off his game.

"Time," the line judge called. "Let's go, boys."

Scott toweled his face and hands. So what weakness did Larry have? Not his serve or his top-spin forehand. Backhand! That was it. He ran around his backhand every chance he got. And he shifted far left or right, trying to take all of Scott's serves on his forehand.

Larry got ready to serve to open the second set. He grinned at Scott. This time Scott grinned back. Now he had a game plan: Play Larry's backhand. Instead of trying to pound each serve back, he would merely block the ball crosscourt into Larry's backhand.

Scott won the first game, and the second, and the third. Larry's face was a mask of confusion. He wasn't playing smart tennis anymore. He was just slamming the ball as hard as he could.

Scott won the second set, 6-2.

The third set was an exciting one. In the final game, Scott lofted a high defensive lob. Larry stalked it, waiting. He wound up for the kill and slammed the ball as hard as he could. It should have been an easy point. Instead, the ball hit the tape, ran along the top of it, then dropped outside the doubles line.

Scott had won the match, 4-6, 6-2, 6-1.

He looked toward the stands. Coach Russo was standing, smiling. He shook his clasped hands above his head. Scott waved his racquet triumphantly and grinned. Then he raised his right hand and, very deliberately, tapped his head with his forefinger. After all, it wasn't a power game. It was a thinking game.

Blind
Ambition

By Marianne Mitchell

"Hey, Jenny. How was your weekend?"

"Oh, fine. And yours?"

"Great!" said Kris, stuffing her books in her locker. "We spent the whole time skiing. You should have seen my crazy brother fly over the moguls."

"No broken legs?"

"So far, so good," said Kris.

Jenny smiled. It was always fun to hear about her friend's adventures with her family. Jenny led a much quieter life. But part of her longed to do something daring—something she could brag about on Monday morning in school.

"Sounds like fun," said Jenny with a sigh. "Since we moved to Colorado, we hear everyone talking about skiing. Wish I could go."

"But you could!" said Kris.

"Are you kidding? Haven't you forgotten something?" asked Jenny.

"What, that you're blind?"

"Yeah. I'd smash into the very first tree."

"Not a chance. Up at Crystal Park, where we ski, there's a program just for skiers who are blind. They've been doing it for years."

"Really? Wow!" Thoughts of going fast, of swishing down the slope, filled Jenny's head. Maybe this was her chance to be a daredevil.

"Why don't you come with us next weekend," urged Kris. "I'll introduce you to one of the instructors. You'll have a blast."

"I . . . I don't know if I could do it," said Jenny.

"Sure you can."

"I'll ask my parents."

On Saturday, Jenny stepped out of the van at Crystal Park. Kris and her family clattered around, unloading all their gear.

Jenny inhaled the icy air laced with the smell of piñon smoke from the lodge. Here she was, ready or not. Could she really go through with this? Kris's words echoed in her mind: "Sure you can."

Kris's family put on their skis, and they headed for the lift line.

"Good luck, Jen!" said Kris's mother. "I called ahead and made arrangements. The instructors are expecting you."

Kris and Jenny crunched their way over the snowy path to the ski school office.

"This is my friend Jenny," said Kris, introducing her. "She has one ambition in life—to ski like the wind."

A firm hand grasped Jenny's. "Welcome to Crystal Park. My name is Britt. I'll be your instructor."

"And guardian angel, I hope," said Jenny with a nervous laugh.

"I'll check with you later," said Kris. "Have fun!"

Jenny knew Kris was eager to join her family on the slopes. Now it was up to her and Britt. Today Jenny would find out how much of a daredevil she really was.

In no time at all, she was fitted with boots, skis, and poles. Britt slipped a silky vest over her head.

"This tells everyone else that you're a skier who's blind. I wear one that says 'Instructor of the Blind.' Everyone gives us the right of way, so don't worry about traffic."

It felt strange sliding along on the skis. In regular shoes, Jenny could feel the ground under her feet. But with heavy boots and skis, she couldn't feel anything. She felt as if she were floating.

They spent most of the morning on the flat areas, getting Jenny used to the skis. She learned how to stand, walk, slide, snowplow, and most important, how to stop. There was even a lesson on falling down.

Britt had a warm and patient voice. She talked Jenny through every move. She had that same "you can do it" attitude that Kris had. Jenny guessed she must be a bit older—sixteen, maybe. After a little practice, Jenny was ready to try her first real slope.

As they waited for the chair lift, Jenny felt a flutter of nerves in her stomach. She took a deep breath. Was she excited or scared? She'd have to trust Britt and listen to her directions.

"We're next," said Britt, guiding her into place. "Get ready to sit. One, two, now!"

Jenny felt the chair bump behind her legs, and she plopped back confidently.

"Super! You act like you've done this all your life," said Britt.

"I wish!" Jenny liked the sensation of riding the lift, swaying a bit as they climbed. The spicy smell of pines told her they were passing over a forest. When they neared the top, Britt gave her the "stand up" cue, then guided her toward the beginner slope.

"Remember, Jenny, when I say turn left, point your knees and ankles left. Point your knees and ankles right for right turns. Keep your weight forward, knees bent."

Jenny pushed off and began to glide down the slope with Britt right beside her.

"You're doing fine!" Britt called to her.

Britt kept up a constant chatter. She told Jenny when to turn, when to slow down, and what the conditions were like.

"We're coming to a nice, gentle run now. Let's go a little faster," said Britt.

"Wow!" cried Jenny. "I can feel the wind in my hair! It's incredible!"

It was a first for Jenny. She'd heard her friends whoosh by on bikes or skateboards. She always wondered what it felt like to have the wind in her hair. Now she knew. It felt great.

They skied the beginner slope three more times that day, stopping only for lunch. With each pass, Jenny grew more confident. For the first time in her life, she felt free—free to do things other kids did, free to dare, free to feel the wind.

At the end of the day, Kris met her at the ski hut. "Well? How was it?"

"Fantastic!" Jenny said with a grin. "You know, you were right. I do want to ski like the wind!"

THE SUPER PLAY

By Ellen A. Kelley

The third quarter of the seventh-grade basket-ball play-off game ends. We're trailing the Slammers by ten. Our starters are tired. With just me and Bryce on the bench, we're shorthanded. Better players like Frankie (Flea) Mora and his pals, Ricky and Jed, have been in for the whole game so far.

Coach signals me. "You and Bryce," he says. "Give Ricky and Jed a break."

We hustle onto the court. I give my glasses a quick polish, figuring this might be my only chance to play today. If there were such a thing as a tenth-string player, I'd be it. I'm not exactly the Sparks' MVP, if you know what I mean.

We've got possession. We look for a chance to score, but the Slammers' defense is a brick wall. You either find a way around it (impossible) or knock your head against it (the usual).

The seconds are dribbling away, but I'm not. Coach yells, "Move your feet! Do something!"

I can't. During practice I know every play as well as I know my name—Julius McGrew. But in a real game my body freezes, afraid it will make a mistake. It just won't do what my brain tells it to.

Coach takes me out.

"Jool-eee-usss," calls Flea. "You're supposed to *pass* the ball. Bryce was wide open."

"Sorry," I say, wishing Flea would leave me alone. But his mouth, like his nickname, is quick, crafty, and ready to bite. In a game, he loves hopping around guards twice his size. Nobody can catch him. He, Jed, and Ricky are the Three Musketeers of basketball. Heck, they could probably have hit three-pointers back in preschool.

"Starters stay in," instructs Coach. They nod, eager to do their duty. And they do it, pounding through the fourth quarter as I watch from the Julius McGrew Memorial Bench.

We score six points, but we're still behind. I wish I could try once more (fat chance). Maybe do things right (not likely).

The next nanosecond my wish is granted. Maynard Loom, the Slammers' biggest guard, sticks his foot out and trips Flea.

Flea falls hard.

"Loooooooooom," sings the crowd, which is packed with Slammers fans. The whistle screeches and the ref calls the foul on Loom.

Flea's lying right in front of me. He doesn't get up. I lean over him. "You OK?"

He opens one eye. His face is the color of dirty ice. "My knee," he whispers. "I'm out."

Coach grabs my arm. "It's up to you," he says.

Who, me? I think, watching them carry Flea to the locker room.

"Nobody can run like Flea," says Ricky, skimming a hand nervously over his flattop and glaring at me.

"Yeah," says Jed. "We're down by four with two minutes left. What'll we do?"

"Push harder, boys," Coach says. "Score. Julius knows the plays."

The guys groan as I unglue my rear from the bench. My hands start to get damp.

"Forget scoring," Jed grumbles.

"Yeah," says Ricky. "Julius never does nothing."

Anything, I silently correct him, but I know he's right.

The clock ticks. Nobody is stupid enough to pass the ball to me. But the Slammers defend like crazy and hold the score.

With one minute left, Loom fouls out. Lucky break for us.

Coach calls time. "Go for the Super Play." He laser-eyes me.

Is he kidding? The Super Play is when Jed steals the ball and passes to Flea. Then Flea breaks away to score while everyone quadruple-guards the Slammers.

But Flea's gone. I'm playing his position. I've *never* made a breakaway basket in my whole life, not even during practice.

The whistle trills. A long Slammer pass and Jed swats the ball—to me! It thuds into my arms. I can't breathe. Or see. Worst of all—I can't think. Slammers are closing in fast.

"Run!" screams Ricky. "GO!"

I go. My legs (whose legs?) wobble downcourt on automatic. My glasses slip down my nose. I trip on my dribbles, but I keep going. I'm afraid a Slammer will catch me, chew me up, and spit me all over the court.

"SHOOT!" bellows Coach.

I stop, look up, and see—our basket! *How did I get down here?* I wonder. Then I shoot.

The ball arcs in slow motion toward the hoop. I'm sure it's short. I'm the short-shot king.

The ball rolls lazily around the rim. Drops in.

I'm shocked. Slammers swarm over me, but they're too late.

The last buzzer buzzes and the game's over. Cheers of happy Slammers fans shatter my tender eardrums.

The Sparks gather around. "Way to go," Ricky says to me.

I don't answer. I'm not used to basketball compliments, especially from the Musketeers.

"Great job," says Coach.

"We still lost," I remind him, "56-54."

"It was a tough game. But *you* won," says Coach. "I've never seen you move like that. What happened to you?"

"I'm not sure. I . . . I couldn't think. Then my feet started moving by themselves."

Coach laughs, glancing up. "Look who's here!"

It's Flea, knee bandaged, leaning on his dad. "I missed everything," he says. "How'd we do?"

"You won't believe this," Ricky and Jed say. Then they high five me, and together, we tell Flea the whole story.

Diary of a
GOLF
FANATIC

By Harriett Diller

JUNE 1. Guess what Uncle J.B. gave me today—me, Susan Amanda Harper—a set of golf clubs! Well, not exactly a set. It's actually Uncle J.B.'s old golf bag and three old clubs. There's a wood—that's for hitting long shots. There's a 5 iron for hitting the in-between shots. There's a putter—that's for using on the green. Now I know what I'm going to do all summer long. I'm going to spend every second at the golf course. P.S.: Uncle J.B. gave me three balls and nine tees, too.

JUNE 2. 8 A.M. How is a golf fanatic supposed to spend every single second at the golf course if her family won't cooperate? At breakfast Mom said she had to take my little brother to his swimming lesson and get groceries and do about a million other unimportant things. Where are her priorities?

10 A.M. I told Mom I'd do five hundred thousand of the million things on her list if she'd drive me to the golf course later. She said she'd think about it.

5 P.M. I made it to the golf course, where I received the shock of my life. You know how easy golf looks on TV? You just hit the ball and it flies straight toward the flag on the green, right? Hah! The first hole on the golf course is a par four. That means you're supposed to get the ball from the tee into the hole on the green by hitting it four times. Guess how many times it took me. One hundred and four!

JUNE 10. What I can't figure out is this: If a wood is for making long shots, how come I never make any long shots with it? I can hit the ball farther with my putter. I'm OK as long as I keep the ball on the ground. But once I try to make it fly— disaster strikes! MORAL FOR THE DAY: IF GOLF BALLS WERE MEANT TO FLY, THEY WOULD HAVE WINGS.

JUNE 21. I found six balls on the golf course. How come people lose so many? Uncle J.B. says I'll understand how, once I learn to hit the ball more than ten yards.

JUNE 28. Today Uncle J.B. took me to the driving range. That's where you practice hitting your long shots (if you have any long shots, that is). Uncle J.B. got me a big bucket of balls and showed me how to swing the wood. One time he said, "Hey, you're supposed to be hitting a golf ball, not digging a garden." Which was kind of impolite of him, but I laughed anyway. Then he showed me how NOT to dig a garden when I hit the ball.

JULY 6. I lost my first ball. Uncle J.B. says I should celebrate. I might if the reason I lost the ball was that I hit it a million yards or something. But the reason I lost it is this (don't tell anybody): I was using my 5 iron to (supposedly) hit onto the green on hole number 8, and instead the ball went sideways into the water on hole number 16. Don't ask me how you can aim straight and hit it sideways. Doesn't that defy the laws of nature or something? P.S.: Uncle J.B. says I had the face of my 5 iron aimed sideways. I didn't even know my 5 iron had a face.

JULY 17. Mom showed me something really neat in the newspaper today. It was an article that said the golf course is offering golf lessons for kids. Mom says I can sign up if I want to.

JULY 28. Uncle J.B. and I practiced on the putting green. Uncle J.B. said, "Don't ever forget—a two-foot putt counts just as much as a two-hundred-yard drive. And even if you can't hit it very far with your driver, you can make it up with your putter."

AUGUST 6. Today I hit the ball into the woods. Every time I tried to hit out of the woods, the ball bounced off a tree and shot right back at me. I got so angry I threw my 5 iron against a tree. It bounced right back, too. MORAL FOR THE DAY: IF PEOPLE WERE MEANT TO PLAY GOLF, THEY WOULDN'T HAVE BEEN GIVEN TEMPERS.

AUGUST 9. I didn't mean what I wrote last time. People are definitely meant to play golf even if they do have tempers. Will somebody please tell my mom this? Uncle J.B. told her about my throwing the 5 iron. She grounded me for three days.

AUGUST 12. I graduated from golf class today. Boy, did I learn a lot about swinging the club and keeping my head down and all sorts of important golf stuff. My teacher said nobody ever really graduates from golf class, not even the pros. There's always something new to learn.

AUGUST 16. Who says balls weren't meant to fly? You should have seen the shot I hit today.

You should have felt how good it was to swing the club through the ball and see the ball fly off. Yes, fly! Well, maybe it didn't go a million yards, but it went farther than I've ever hit one before. It was beautiful.

AUGUST 24. My birthday! And guess what my present was—my own set of golf clubs. I can't wait to get to the golf course and try them. But Mom says she has to take my little brother to the dentist and to shop for school clothes, and then she has to do a million other unimportant things before she can take me. Maybe I'll offer to do five hundred thousand of them for her. Or maybe I'll do the whole million.

The Winners

By Joan Strauss

Amy sent a ball spinning down the alley for the winning point. She ran to the net and pretended to jump over it, but of course she was too short. The girls on the other side of the court laughed, as she intended.

She grinned at Lisa, her doubles partner. "If we play like this in the tournament, we've got it made."

They reached across the net to shake hands with their opponents. Kathy, the recreation council coach, insisted on that, even in practice.

"Don't be too sure," Lisa cautioned. "I know you think you're going to be a great tennis player, but a lot of those kids in the tournament belong to tennis clubs. They play every day, all year round."

"Good work, girls," Kathy told them. "Amy, get more snap into that serve. And Lisa, don't forget the follow-through on your backhand."

She consulted her clipboard. "The recreation council championships start this Saturday morning at nine at Franklin Park. See you there, girls. And good luck!"

Friends since third grade, Amy and Lisa had learned tennis together in the public parks program. Although small for their age, they took to tennis like pros. This year, they had earned the doubles spot for their division in the championships.

"I'll bet we'll be playing on the singles team in another year," Amy boasted.

"First, we've got some doubles players to beat," Lisa warned.

When they arrived at Franklin Park for the tournament, neither one was certain of their chances. Hard-hitting girls and guys were already practicing, powering their serves over the net. Others sat on the grass watching and talking together, looking sure of themselves in their fancy tennis clothes.

"Hi, girls." It was Kathy. "You play on court number three after the singles matches."

Amy walked to the court swinging her racquet and flourishing her forehand. Lisa knew Amy always clowned around when she was nervous.

She had good reason to be nervous. Their opponents, Jennifer and Diana, were two tall girls in crisp tennis whites, older and certainly more at ease than Lisa and Amy.

Lisa shook her head at Amy. "No more fooling around." But Amy strutted onto the tennis court, still showing off.

As they took their positions, they heard a snicker and a remark from the other side of the court. "Little kids from the public playground. We'll wipe up the courts with them. Let's meet at the club later for some *real* tennis."

Lisa took one look at her friend's face. Amy narrowed her eyes and marched toward the baseline to start the match.

Jennifer and Diana played in a graceful, leisurely manner, while Amy and Lisa doggedly concentrated on everything Kathy had taught them. At the end of the first set, Jennifer and Diana were surprised to find themselves behind, 6-3.

They began to play in earnest, angling shots crosscourt and slamming balls from the net position. Amy and Lisa fought back. Jennifer and Diana took the second set, 6-4, but most of the games went to deuce before the older team could end them.

"Do you think we can take 'em?" Lisa asked Amy at the water fountain during the break before the last set of the match.

Amy looked at Kathy, who was sitting with the girls' mothers, watching. She gave Amy a thumbs-up sign.

"Even if we can't, we're not going to make it easy for 'em," Amy answered, her mouth set in a determined line.

The other team wasn't taking any chances. They gave up the flashy stuff and played solid tennis. Rising to the challenge, Amy and Lisa returned shot for shot, but Jennifer and Diana were more seasoned competitors.

As the tide started to turn in their direction, the older girls began to taunt the younger players.

"Having a little trouble?" drawled Diana.

"That's what happens when you play with the big kids," added Jennifer.

That was all Amy and Lisa needed. Slowly, they started to win games again, until the score stood at five games each. A crowd had gathered to watch, but Amy and Lisa didn't notice. The taunts stopped, but their opponents ran them all over the court mercilessly.

Experience and strength began to pay off. Jennifer and Diana hammered out point after point to win the last two games, the set, and the match.

"Thought you had us, didn't you?" Diana sneered when they all shook hands over the net.

Amy and Lisa stayed cool. They had fought the battle on the court with the best tennis they had ever played.

Walking off, Lisa copied Amy's confident swing at an imaginary forehand.

Amy grinned at her. "Good work."

"You, too," Lisa answered.

It was funny. They had lost, but somehow they felt as if they had won.

Underhand

By David Dayen

Frankie went up for the rebound. He caught the ball on the way down and jumped back up to take a shot. But the defender slapped him on the arm.

The referee blew the whistle. "Foul, number 32, green. Two shots."

Frankie gazed up at the scoreboard. He took a deep breath. This was the part he hated the most. Free throws.

It wasn't that Frankie was a poor shooter. He was probably as good as any shooter on his team.

But something happened whenever he stepped up to the line during a game. He'd get very nervous. His nose would start to twitch like a mouse smelling fresh cheese. His palms would sweat. He would never be able to focus on the rim. And more often than not, he would miss the shot.

Sure enough, when Frankie let his first foul shot fly, the ball sailed short. It didn't even hit the rim.

"Air ball, air ball," the fans of the other team chanted. Frankie cast his eyes downward.

His coach clapped his hands and yelled out instructions to his player. "How about underhand style, Frankie?"

Frankie widened his eyes. The coach had pulled him aside last week in practice and tried to teach him a new shooting approach. He had Frankie hold the ball in front of his legs, with his hands on either side of it and his feet spread apart. Then he had Frankie throw the ball toward the hoop.

Frankie seemed to take to this underhand style. At one point, he made ten in a row. But when the other kids on the team watched Frankie practice, they laughed. "You shoot like a baby," one of them said.

The coach quickly scolded Frankie's teammates. "Wilt Chamberlain shot that way. Rick Barry shot that way. You think anybody called those super-stars a baby? Besides, as long as the ball goes in the net, who cares how it gets there?" But that didn't stop the team from teasing Frankie in private.

While he stood at the line, Frankie thought, *No way I'm shooting underhanded.* He concentrated on the basket, aiming the ball for the center. Knees shaking, Frankie tossed the ball. It clanked off the back of the rim, falling harmlessly into an opponent's hands. Frankie kicked at the hardwood. The coach called a time-out.

The coach pulled Frankie aside during the break. "Why didn't you use the underhand shot? We worked on it all week."

"Aw, Coach, please don't make me do that," pleaded Frankie. He picked up a towel from the bench and wiped the sweat from his face.

Coach looked at him and shook his head, frowning. Frankie looked at the scoreboard again. His team was losing by a point with only a few seconds to play.

The coach set up the defense in the huddle, instructing Frankie and his teammate Eddie to immediately guard whoever gets the ball and try to get a steal.

And that's just what happened. The other team inbounded to their point guard in the corner, and

Frankie and Eddie trapped him there. The point guard tried to pass the ball, but Frankie batted it in the air and caught it on its way down. The clock was running down. Frankie dribbled toward the basket. He was about to attempt a lay-up when an opposing player held his arm. Once again, the referee blew the whistle and called a foul. Frankie had to go to the free-throw line again, this time with a chance to win the game.

Frankie looked around the gym, unsure of himself. Should he shoot underhanded? What if he missed? Not only would his team lose the game, but he would look like a baby as well. But as Frankie approached the foul line, he knew that if he shot underhanded, he would have a better chance of scoring. He glanced at the coach, who clapped his hands and stared at Frankie. "You know what to do, Frankie," the coach hollered across the court.

The referee tossed the ball to Frankie. Frankie twirled the ball in his hands, bouncing it on the floor a couple of times. He looked up at the basket. It seemed so far away. Frankie swallowed hard.

Frankie spread his feet far apart, just like in practice. To him, nobody else was in the gym. It was just him and the hoop. Frankie bent his knees and tossed the ball high in the air. It softly settled through the basket, tickling the white netting as it fell. Tie score!

Frankie looked toward his bench to see if his teammates were laughing. But everybody on the bench cheered wildly. Frankie returned his focus to the basket. One more foul shot and the game was theirs. Frankie used the same crouch and fol-low-through that was successful the last time. And the ball fluttered through the basket with a perfect SWISH. The buzzer sounded. Frankie had won the game!

Frankie's team mobbed him as he stood at the free-throw line. The coach wedged his way in through his players and whispered to Frankie, "I'm proud of you."

Frankie knew that the coach was right. As long as the ball goes in the net, who cares how it gets there?

The Tarantula

By Ellen A. Kelley

It was the last minute of the game—we needed to score a goal.

I looked up. Spotted the goalie. Stopped. Gasped. Gagged. Felt sweat drips running down my neck. This was no goalie. It was a giant tarantula!

"Help!" I screamed.

"Score!" the crowd screamed back. Were they kidding? Even under normal circumstances, I'm no star. Just Matt Mendoza, Mr. Average. I was helpless against this overgrown spider guarding the goal.

The monster crept out to get me. I couldn't run. My feet were tangled in a web. The spider crept closer. Opened its huge mouth. Breathed its hot breath on my face . . .

Then I woke up from the worst nightmare of my life.

I checked the clock, untangled my feet from the sheets, and saw that I had one hour until the *second* worst nightmare of my life. Only this time it wouldn't be a dream.

Today we were playing the Jets. We were closely matched except for one thing: their goalie, Bobby Brusco. Bobby is the biggest fifth-grader in the county. Because of Bobby, no one has scored against the Jets all season.

Bobby's dark hair hangs in his face, so you can't see his eyes. But he can see you. The ball never gets past Bobby. His arms and legs are everywhere. He jumps on the ball as if it's some little fly to munch for supper. That's why they call him . . . the Tarantula.

"It's time to go," Mom yelled.

"Coming," I yelled back.

"We're late," she said.

"OK," I said, grabbing my soccer jersey.

"You don't look so good," Mom said when I got in the van. "Feeling all right?"

"No," I said. "I feel awful. We're going to lose, and all because of that spider guy."

"What spider? What guy? What are you talking about?" she said.

"Their goalie," I said, "the Tarantula. We'll never get the ball past him. I know it. It won't be a pretty sight, Mom."

"Try to have a more positive attitude," Mom said as we pulled into the parking lot. She handed me my water bottle. "Good luck."

"Thanks," I muttered, and trudged to the bench.

The game went just as I thought it would. We played really hard, and they didn't score. But even Megan, our best forward, couldn't kick the ball past the Tarantula.

After three quarters my throat was as dry as dust. I grabbed my water bottle. The game was nearly over, so I gulped until the bottle was empty.

We struggled back and forth until about one minute remained, then Megan finally broke loose. She passed me the ball in the center of the field, and I raced toward the goal, expecting to hear the final whistle.

But then I reached the goal, face-to-face with the Tarantula. He crouched with his arms wide apart in front of him, facing the ball as I approached. The crowd was shouting "Score!"

I planted my left foot and got ready to fire the ball with all my might. And then it happened.

A gurgle in my stomach quickly rose in a bubble that burst out of my mouth in one big burp. An enormous burp. A King Kong burp.

The Tarantula laughed. He laughed hard. And for that one split second, he looked away from the ball.

My foot connected with the ball, and it rocketed toward the corner of the goal. The Tarantula leaped for it but missed. Goal! The game was over. We'd beaten the best team in the county!

My teammates slapped me on the back, and Coach yelled, "Way to go, Mendoza!" I was the star.

I was walking back to our van when the Tarantula caught up with me.

"Hey," he said. The Tarantula could talk! "You forgot something."

"What?" I asked.

"You're supposed to say 'excuse me'," he said with a smile. He shook my hand. Then he walked away, still grinning.

"Was that the Tarantula?" Mom asked as she unlocked the van.

"No," I said. I could see him on the field with his coach. They were both laughing. "That was Bobby Brusco."

The Great
Snow-Pudding
Race

By Diane Burns

Adam is bunched in the front of our racing sled, like a fur-hooded marshmallow with leg braces. He grips the sled's hand controls. His wide-open mouth catches falling globs of snow. "It's thick like pudding, Jeff. Snow pudding!"

The falling snow is thick all right, so thick it hides the crowd. Still, we hear their cheers, and the race hasn't even started. Everyone from the Rehab Center is here, all the workers and patients, and they are cheering loud enough to start an avalanche. We hear Miss Chelsea, our teacher from therapy class who taught us to swim last summer. She showed us how to race this special sled, too.

Her voice is big and kind. "Go, Adam and Jeff! Think of the doughnut, not the hole!"

That's her favorite way of telling us to think about good things, not bad things. But thinking of good things today won't be easy. Adam and I will try to steer around four red flags while we race downhill on our sled. Three other teams will steer around their colored flags at the same time.

The blowing snow makes racing tough. It hides the other teams and their flags. It hides *our* flags. It even hides the bottom of the hill. Maybe the hill has no bottom.

Adam looks at me with wide eyes. We've never sledded in falling snow before. Can we do it? Suppose we get lost? Suppose we tip over? We'd be stranded! No one is allowed to lift us back onto the sled today, the way they could during practice runs.

"It's hard to think about the doughnut and not the hole," Adam whimpers.

Adam knows what I'm thinking. There's so much to watch and remember, like steering and balance. And now doughnuts on top of it all.

BANG! The starting gun makes us jump.

"Go! Go!" shouts the crowd.

"Go, Red Team!" cheers Miss Chelsea.

Adam and I push our mittened hands against the snowy ground. Our sled jumps forward. Faster and faster it goes. We spot something red through the blowing snow. Our first flag! Adam steers the sled smoothly around the stick.

Our sled shoots downhill. Where is the second red flag?

"Over there, over there," Adam chants. We head in the direction of his pointing mitten, into the icy wind.

Snow stings our faces. There's no sound now except for the swish of our sled. The storm has swallowed the crowd in its huge, white mouth. It's swallowed the other racers. Us, too.

We skim around the second flag. The pudding snow whirls and swirls. There's our third flag! We steer hard toward it. Too hard. The sled dumps over.

Adam flails helplessly in the thick snow. I wish I had something to grab, even my wheelchair. I feel buried in my big parka, like a turtle in its shell. Hey! "Pretend you're a turtle, Adam," I call.

He sees me pounding the snowy ground with my arms, then dragging my legs behind. It's hard work.

Finally, my boot bumps the sled and tips it upright. I reach toward Adam with one mittened hand, but Adam isn't playing turtle anymore.

"I'm tired and cold," he grumps. "The wind hurts." He rolls onto his back and folds his arms across his chest. "Get Miss Chelsea!"

Pulling us back onto the sled won't be easy. And hurtling downhill into the storm again will be scary. But I want to keep trying. And I know Adam does, too.

"Remember the doughnut," I pant, pushing Adam onto the sled, "not the . . . "

". . . hole," Adam finishes. His eyebrows are caked with snow. He looks exactly like a frightened snowman.

I flop into the front and reach for the steering controls. "Stay low behind me, out of the wind."

Adam's leg braces clamp around my waist, like a hug. He takes a deep breath. I know he is thinking about our race and the snow and the wind. He wipes snow from his cheek. He takes another deep breath.

"OK," he says.

Our sled races into the thick, white pudding once more.

The wind freezes our breath; it numbs our fingers and toes.

Maybe this hill really doesn't have a bottom. Maybe we'll zoom on and on forever. Drat those doughnut-hole thoughts! Then—

Hurrah! There's the last red flag! We steer around it and fly downhill. We're at the bottom, across the finish line. Safe!

We brake, and the sled spills us again, this time near the cheering crowd. There's snow in my mouth, but that's OK. Adam is swimming in the snow and hollering loud enough for both of us.

"Let's do it again. Hurray for snow pudding!"

I know Adam. I know what's coming next. I swallow my mouthful of snow, and we chant together:

"Hurray for doughnuts!"

ITCHING TO PLAY

By Ellen A. Kelley

All week I'd been thinking about the championship game.

My best friend, Crystal, and I had talked about how we'd get our picture in the sports section, and how we might even be recruited for the United States Olympic women's basketball team.

"This kid Emma Crookshank is star material," the scout would say. "Keep an eye on her."

The more I thought about it, the more I realized that my future could depend on this game.

I woke up at dawn on Saturday morning. I was so nervous, it felt as if a hundred grasshoppers were slam-dunking basketballs in my stomach.

But when I glanced in the mirror, I knew I had a problem—a big problem. I went back to bed and lay there, wondering what to do.

Ten minutes later my parents came in. I hid under the covers. "Hey, champ," my father said. "It's 8:00. Pre-game practice starts at 9:30. You'd better hustle!"

I pulled the covers tighter over my head and scrunched into a ball.

"What's going on?" I heard my mother ask. She's a registered nurse. I stayed in the same position and said nothing.

"She's probably got butterflies in her stomach," she said to my father.

I moaned.

"I'll tell you what she's got," said my father. "She's got an attitude." He pulled my pillow out from under my head. "Just because she's the star of the team, she thinks she can stay in bed all morning."

I groaned. I wished I had butterflies. I wished I had an attitude. I wished I didn't have what I had, which was much, much worse. I unscrunched, sat up, and looked at my parents. "I've got some kind of disease," I said.

I pulled up my pajama top so they could see for themselves. My stomach was covered with itchy red bumps. There were more bumps on my arms and legs, and even a few on my face. I felt hot and cold at the same time, and I looked like an alien from the planet Pimple.

"Chicken pox," my mother said. "Let's take your temperature." She went to the hall closet for the thermometer. "Who have you been around?" she asked, sticking the thermometer under my tongue.

"Humpf-wheff," I answered.

"There goes the game," said my father. "I'll call your coach."

"Wait a minute," I said, pulling the thermometer out of my mouth. "Don't call her. I'll take some medicine. I'll be fine. I've got to play!" My father waited in the doorway.

"Call the coach," my mother told him. "You can't play," she said to me. "You're contagious. Take your pajamas off and meet me in the bathroom." I felt too sick to argue.

Two minutes later, I stood in my robe and watched my mother fill the bathtub with water. Then she dumped in about a half a box of stuff labeled oatmeal powder.

"Wait a minute," I said, scratching my belly. "I hate oatmeal. It tastes like a dusty old sock."

My mother stirred the cereal with her hand until the water turned gray. "You're not going to eat it," she said. "You're going to bathe in it."

I stared at her and scratched the bumps on my elbow. "You mean I have to sit in that?"

She nodded. "It should help the itching. Now get in before your oatmeal gets cold."

Later that morning I lay on the couch in the living room. The game was scheduled to start in about an hour. I felt useless just lying there, knowing that the team needed me.

I tried watching TV to take my mind off things, but it didn't help. I felt as if I were in a sweltering jungle, with 10,000 mosquito bites covering me. My mother came in and dabbed lotion on me. "I can't believe I'm missing the game," I said.

"Things happen, Emma," she said.

"I'll bet nothing like this ever happens to the pros," I said.

"Things happen to *everyone*," she answered. "And stop exaggerating."

The phone rang. It was Crystal. "Coach just called me," she said. "How are you feeling?" Her voice sounded tight.

"Oh, just super," I snarled. "How would you feel if you messed up the most important game of the whole season?"

"You don't have to yell about it," Crystal said. "It isn't my fault you caught the chicken pox."

Then Crystal hung up on me.

I punched my fist into the pillow.

"Calm down," my mother said from the hallway. "You have another call."

"I don't want to talk to anybody," I said.

"It's your coach," she said. "She wants to talk with you." My mother handed me the phone.

"Hey, Emma. How are you doing?" It was the coach all right, and she didn't sound angry at all.

"OK, I guess."

"Well, it turns out you're not the only one with the chicken pox," she said.

"I'm not?"

"Nope. Three other girls showed up at practice with red polka dots. The game is postponed for two weeks. So get well soon."

Get well? I'd never felt better in my life. We would dazzle the crowd for sure. We'd capture every rebound, make every free throw. Olympic scouts would discover us. And we would win.

The doorbell yanked me out of my daydream. There was Crystal. "It's OK," she told me. "I've already had chicken pox. You look awful," she said, grinning, and gave me a high five.

"Thanks," I said, and I gave her a high five back.

Tough Call

By Suzanne Rzeznikiewicz

Kelly placed the awkward-fitting blue batting helmet on her head and stepped up to the plate.

"Please let me get a hit this time," she whispered to herself.

The pitcher threw the ball. Kelly watched it go past her.

"Strike one!" called the umpire.

I better swing at this next one, thought Kelly, and she tightened her grip on the bat. The ball came at her.

"Strike two!" It was just a little too high, Kelly realized after she had swung.

Kelly thought of her father and mother in the stands. She almost wished they didn't come to her baseball games. It was so embarrassing for them to see her strike out all the time. They never said anything, of course, but Kelly knew they must be disappointed in her.

The pitcher checked the bases, turned to face Kelly, then swung his arm forward and threw a perfect pitch right over the plate.

"Strike three!" yelled the umpire.

Kelly walked, head down, back to her team's bench, dragging the bat behind her.

It wasn't that she didn't like baseball. She loved it. She just wasn't very good at it. It didn't help that Kelly was a lefty. The few times she did hit the ball it rolled right to the first baseman, and Kelly was tagged out.

"All right, let's go on that field and get them out one, two, three!" encouraged Coach Miller. "Mary, you're pitching. Brian, take second. Kelly, you're left field."

The second half of the inning went by quickly— one pop fly, one strike out, and a tag at first. It wasn't long before Kelly's team was up at bat again.

"You're up next, Kelly," said Coach Miller.

OK, Kelly said to herself as she stood on deck. *Here's your chance.*

"Batter up!"

Kelly took her place and faced the pitcher. Her hands gripped the bat tightly and her heart pounded in her chest. She saw the ball coming toward her, closed her eyes and swung.

"Strike one!"

"Keep your eye on the ball, Kelly," encouraged Coach Miller from the bench.

"Come on, Kelly. Get a hit. You can do it!" yelled her teammates.

Kelly took a deep breath and faced the pitcher again. The ball flew toward her. This time Kelly kept her eyes open. Kelly watched and watched and then swung.

SMACK! Kelly had gotten a hit! She watched the ball head just to the right of the pitcher. Kelly dropped the bat and ran as fast as she could to first base. The pitcher scooped up the ball and threw.

"Safe!" yelled the umpire.

Kelly almost jumped up and down with glee. She was on base! She had made it! She looked toward the stands and grinned at her parents. Her father and mother grinned back.

The next batter stepped up to the plate. Kelly took a few steps lead. The batter hit the ball and

Kelly ran toward second. She could hear people yelling and clapping as she ran. Kelly wondered whether they were clapping for her or the batter or the other team. The ball was picked up by the shortstop and thrown to the second baseman. The second baseman caught the ball as Kelly ran past her. Kelly felt the tag on her back just seconds before her foot landed on the bag. She felt her heart sink. Kelly knew she was out.

"Safe!" yelled the umpire.

The crowd in the stands responded with more clapping and shouting.

All right! thought Kelly. *He called me safe. I can stay on base. Maybe I'll even make it home!*

"Wait a minute!" protested the second baseman. "I tagged her. She's out."

"No, she was safe," said the shortstop.

The umpire nodded, then indicated they should start playing again. The second baseman kicked at the dirt, her head lowered.

Kelly looked at the second baseman standing near her. She thought of her parents watching her. Most of all she thought about how she loved standing on second base and how much she wanted to make it all the way home.

Without warning she heard herself say, "I was out. She tagged me out."

Kelly felt her feet carrying her off the field. Her head was down and her stomach felt funny. Had she done the right thing? Was her coach going to be angry? What would her parents think?

Then Kelly heard clapping, lots of clapping, coming from the bleachers. She looked up. They were all clapping for her! Some people were even standing. Kelly saw her parents smile. Her father flashed her a thumbs-up sign. When Kelly reached the bench, Coach Miller patted her on the back and said, "Good job, Kelly."

Kelly smiled at her and said, "Next time I'm up at bat maybe I'll make it to third base!"

Learning to
FISH

By Sarah Anne Shope

Andrea stepped down onto the flat rock at the water's edge. It would make a good place to sit while she and Grandma fished. She smiled to herself as she thought about the big fish she wanted to catch for dinner.

Quickly, Andrea baited her hook. Then she threw the line into the water.

"Oh no!" Andrea shouted. She looked at the tangled line on her reel.

Suddenly, her rod jerked. "I've got a great big fish!" she said with excitement.

"You had better reel him in," Grandma called.

Andrea looked over at the gray-haired woman. "I can't. My line is tangled."

"Let me help."

Soon the line was untangled, and Grandma handed it back. "Here." She smiled. "Now, next time make sure your reel is working right."

Andrea started to smile back. Then she noticed the line lying still. "My fish is gone," she said sadly. "I'll never learn to catch fish."

Grandma sat down on the rock beside Andrea. "Here, try again. Maybe I can help you."

"But I can't do anything right." Andrea's face looked angry. She slammed the rod down.

"Patience, dear," Grandma said. "Here, let me show you how to cast."

Soon, with a little help, Andrea was fishing again. Together Andrea and Grandma sat on the rock and talked and fished.

"How come you always catch so many fish?" Andrea asked curiously.

"Well, I don't always catch them. Sometimes they outsmart me."

Andrea laughed. "Fish aren't smarter than people."

"Oh, sometimes they are. People get angry, and they get impatient, too. Sometimes they make too much noise and scare the fish away."

"But fishing is easy," Andrea said.

"Not always. You have to learn where to fish, when to fish, and how to fish," her grandmother said. "The fish only have to learn one thing: how to eat your worms without swallowing the hook." They both laughed.

Suddenly, Andrea felt another nibble. On her feet, she shouted and jerked the line. She reeled it in as fast as she could. An empty hook came out of the water.

"What did I do wrong?" she asked angrily.

"Well, maybe you jerked the line too soon. You have to give the fish a chance to take the hook," Grandma explained.

Andrea's anger quickly went away. "I guess the fish outsmarted me again. I wonder if fish ever get impatient and angry."

She baited her hook again. Carefully, she cast it out into the lake. She smiled at her grandmother.

"Now you're learning to fish, Andrea," the woman said softly. Andrea and Grandma smiled at each other.